Level 2

DreamWorks

HOW TO TRAIN YOUR DRAGON 2

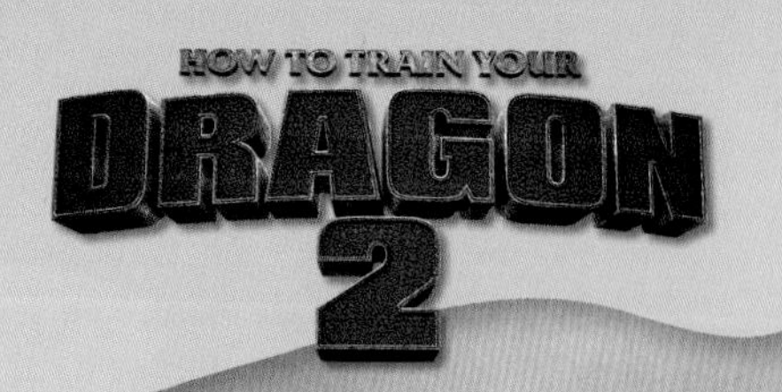

The Vikings of Berk

These Vikings live on the island of Berk. They love their dragons.

Hiccup flies everywhere on his dragon, Toothless.

Hiccup

Astrid is Hiccup's girlfriend. She flies with him to new places.

Astrid

Stoick

Stoick is Hiccup's dad and a Viking chief.

DRAGONS

Toothless is Hiccup's dragon.

Alpha dragons are very strong. All dragons obey them. Valka and Drago have Alpha dragons.

Valka

Valka is Hiccup's mum, but she doesn't live with him.

Drago wants all Vikings and dragons to obey him. He has a dragon army.

Eret works for Drago. He captures dragons for Drago's army.

Drago

Eret

Before you read …

What do you think? Where does Valka live?

New Words

What do these new words mean? Ask your teacher or use your dictionary.

capture

They **captured** the animals.

army

People in the **army** have to wear green and brown.

chief

Everyone listened to the **chief**.

attack

The dog is **attacking** the girl.

fight / fighter

The girls are **fighting**. They are good **fighters**.

island

It is an **island**.

kill

A cat **killed** a small animal.

obey

The dog **obeyed**.

save

ship

They went on a **ship**.

'Let us go!'

Verbs

Present	Past
fly	flew
fight	fought
take	took

CHAPTER ONE
A new land

Hiccup was a young Viking. He lived with his dad, Stoick, on the island of Berk. A long time ago, dragons were a big problem, but now Vikings and dragons never fought. Hiccup loved his dragon, Toothless.

Hiccup was with Astrid and their dragons.

They flew away from Berk. 'Look, Astrid! A new land,' Hiccup said. 'Let's go and see it.'

Hiccup looked down and saw a Viking ship. The Vikings wanted to capture their dragons!

'Stop! What are you doing?' Hiccup shouted.

'I'm Eret,' cried one of the Vikings. 'I capture dragons for Drago's army.'

Eret attacked, but Hiccup and Astrid flew away on their dragons.

'Drago is going to take all your dragons!' Eret shouted after them.

Back on Berk, Hiccup talked to his dad, the Viking chief.

'Drago has a dragon army?' Stoick asked. 'Help me save Berk!'

But Hiccup wanted to talk to Drago first.

'You can't talk to Drago,' Stoick said. 'He's a very bad man.'

CHAPTER TWO
'Who are you?'

Hiccup wanted to think. He flew away on Toothless.

Suddenly, there was a woman on a dragon next to him. She took Hiccup to her island. There were dragons everywhere!

'Who are you?' Hiccup asked the woman.

'I'm Valka – your mum.'

'My mum?' Hiccup asked.

'Yes, Hiccup,' Valka said. 'I came here a long time ago because I wanted to help the dragons. I live here with them. My Alpha dragon is my teacher. All the dragons here obey him.'

'Everyone was frightened of dragons on Berk, so they attacked them,' Valka said.

'But we don't attack dragons now,' Hiccup said. 'They're our friends. We all fly on dragons!'

Valka laughed happily.

CHAPTER THREE
'Take us to Drago!'

Astrid and her friends looked for Hiccup on their dragons. Suddenly, Astrid saw Eret's ship.

'Take us to Drago!' Astrid shouted.

'No!' Eret cried, but Astrid's dragon took Eret from the ship.

'OK!' Eret said angrily.

On Drago's island, his men captured them.

'Let us go!' Astrid shouted to Drago. 'Hiccup is looking for us. He's a great fighter with a very strong dragon.'

Drago laughed. 'I have a dragon army. I'm going to attack Berk and capture all the dragons.'

Stoick looked for Hiccup too. He came to an island with many dragons. Suddenly, he saw Hiccup.

'I'm here to save you. Come with me!' Stoick cried.

Then Stoick saw Valka.

'Are you angry with me, Stoick?' Valka said. 'I ran away because I wanted to help the dragons.'

'No! I loved you then and I love you now,' Stoick said.

'Please come back to Berk with your dragons, mum!' Hiccup said.

'Yes!' Valka answered.

Stoick took Valka's arm and they danced. Valka's dragons flew around them

Suddenly, they saw Drago's ships and his army.

'Drago's attacking! Save the dragons!' Valka cried.

Drago was on his ship. 'I'm going to attack Valka's Alpha dragon,' he shouted. 'Then all of the dragons are going to obey mine.'

CHAPTER FOUR
Toothless obeys

Astrid and her friends fought Drago's men. Eret fought with them.

All the dragons fought too.

Drago's Alpha dragon was very strong. It killed Valka's Alpha dragon.

'No!' Hiccup cried.

Now all the dragons obeyed Drago's Alpha dragon. And the Alpha Dragon obeyed Drago!

Hiccup wanted to stop the fighting.

'Why are you attacking us and our dragons?' he asked Drago.

'I want all dragons everywhere to obey me,' Drago said.

Now Toothless obeyed the Alpha dragon.

'Kill Hiccup!' Drago shouted to Toothless.

Toothless started to obey.

'No!' Stoick shouted. He jumped in front of Hiccup and saved him.

'Go away, Toothless!' Hiccup shouted.

'Toothless obeyed Drago and his Alpha dragon, Hiccup,' Valka said. 'When they obey bad dragons, good dragons can do bad things.'

'To Berk!' Drago shouted to his men. 'Let's go!'

All the dragons flew after Drago.

CHAPTER FIVE
A new Alpha dragon

'How can we go to Berk and stop Drago?' Astrid asked Hiccup. 'All the dragons went with him.'

'There are some young dragons here,' said Hiccup. 'They don't obey Alpha dragons. We can fly on them.'

'Let's go!' said Astrid.

On Berk, Drago's Alpha dragon looked at the young dragons, not at the Vikings or the Viking's dragons.

Hiccup saw Toothless. 'Wake up, my friend! Come back to me!' he shouted.

Slowly, Toothless went to Hiccup.

Now Toothless fought the Alpha dragon. The dragons watched. Toothless was small, but very strong. Then the dragons came to him and fought with him.

'This is the end!' Hiccup shouted to Drago.

'No!' Drago answered. 'Fight!' he shouted to his Alpha dragon.

But the Alpha dragon didn't obey. It went away and took Drago with him.

All the dragons obeyed Toothless now.

'Toothless is the new Alpha dragon!' said Hiccup.

The Vikings ran happily to their dragons.

'Thank you Hiccup! Thank you Toothless!' they shouted.

THE END

The Vikings

Who were the Vikings?

They were people from Norway, Sweden and Denmark. A long time ago (about 790 AD to 1066 AD), they travelled by sea to new places. Some Vikings stayed in the new places. Many traded with people there and then went home.

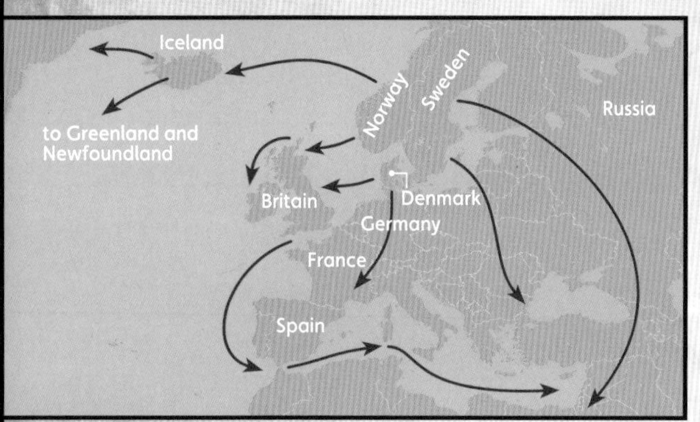

A Viking family

Viking homes

Many Vikings lived in longhouses. A lot of people lived in a longhouse and their animals lived there too. One longhouse in Lofoten, Norway, was 83m long!

Viking longships

There were many Viking ships. Some were for trade, but some were for travel or for fighting. These ships were long and very quick.

Many longships had carvings of dragons on them. People in England called these ships 'dragonships'. They were frightened of the dragon carvings.

Would you like to be a Viking? Why / Why not?

What do these words mean? Find out.

people trade travel carving call

After you read

1 Answer these questions. Write the names.

a) Who is Hiccup's girlfriend? ....Astrid....

b) Who is Hiccup's dad? ....

c) Who is Hiccup's mum? ....

d) What is the name of Hiccup's dragon? ....

e) Who is the Viking chief? ....

f) Who captures dragons? ....

g) Who has a dragon army? ....

2 True (✓) or False (✗)? Write in the box.

a) The Vikings on Berk don't love dragons. ☒

b) Dragons can live happily with people. ☐

c) Dragons can fly. ☐

d) Dragons obey Alpha dragons. ☐

e) Valka doesn't like dragons. ☐

f) Drago wants to attack Berk. ☐

g) Baby dragons obey Alpha dragons. ☐

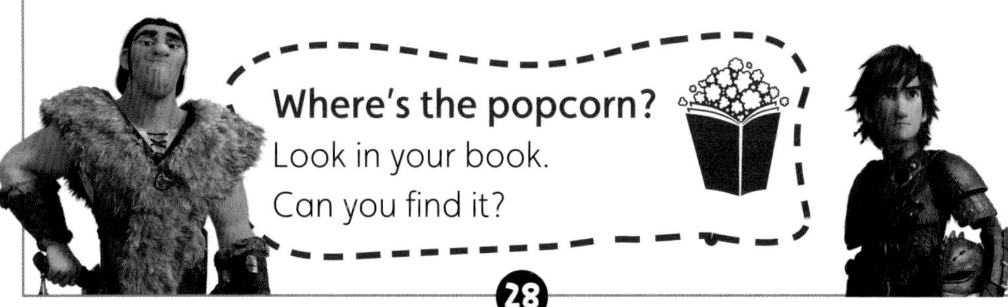

Puzzle time!

1 Colour the dragon. Then write the colours.

2 Do the maze. Which dragon goes to the island?

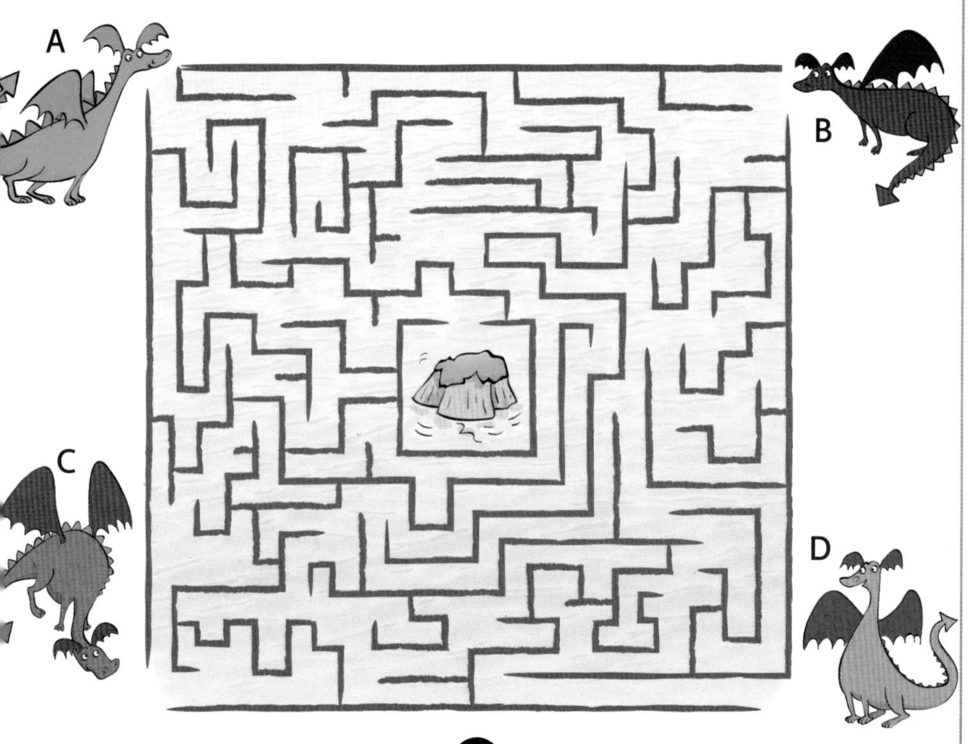

3a Complete the words.

1 not good: b a d
2 not short: __ a l l
3 not cold: h o __
4 not end: s t __ r t
5 not laugh: __ r y
6 not run: w a l __

b Now write the words in the dragon. What word do the letters spell?

Imagine ...

1 Choose a character. Write three things about him, her or it.

....

....

....

2 Tell your friends the three things. Who are you? Do they know?

I love dragons.
My Alpha dragon was my teacher. I am a mum, I'm going to live in Berk again.

You're Valka!

Chant

1 Listen and read.

Stoick and Valka

Valka, oh Valka, don't stay away.
We're friends with our dragons. Come, see them play.
I'm the great chief of Berk now. Hiccup and I say:
'Come back and live with us. Come back and stay.'

Stoick, oh Stoick, I hear and understand.
Take me back to Berk. Let me take your hand.
Dragons are our friends, quick, slow, big or small.
We can fly and laugh with them. We can love them all.

2  Say the chant.